A & M

forever...

SIMON & SCHUSTER BOOKS FOR YOUNG READERS
An imprint of Simon & Schuster Children's Publishing Division
1230 Avenue of the Americas, New York, New York 10020
Copyright © 2005 by Mandy Stanley
First published in Great Britain in 2005 by HarperCollins Publishers Ltd.
First U.S. edition 2006
SIMON & SCHUSTER BOOKS FOR YOUNG READERS is a trademark of Simon & Schuster, Inc.
The text for this book is set in Bernhard Gothic.
Printed & bound in China by Imago
2 4 6 8 10 9 7 5 3 1
Library of Congress Cataloging-in-Publication Data
Stanley, Mandy.
Lettice the flower girl / Mandy Stanley.— 1st U.S. ed.
p. cm.
Summary: Lettice has the honor of being the flower girl at her dance teacher's wedding.
ISBN-13: 978-1-4169-1157-9 (isbn 13)
ISBN-10: 1-4169-1157-X (isbn 10)
[1. Weddings—Fiction. 2. Rabbits—Fiction.] I. Title.
PZ7.S78925Ldy 2006
[E]—dc22
2005007668

Lettice

The Flower Girl

Mandy Stanley

Simon & Schuster Books for Young Readers
New York London Toronto Sydney

One day Lettice popped her head out of her burrow and saw a letter fluttering on a bush. "It's for ME!" she squeaked.

Lettice

Paws shaking, Lettice opened the letter.
It said:

Dear Lettice,
I am getting married very soon.
Will you be my flower girl?
Come and see me today and I'll tell you all about it.
Love,
Your dance teacher
Giselle xxx

Lettice wiggled with excitement. A flower girl!

She scampered over the hill
to her dance teacher's house.

"Come in, Lettice," said Giselle,
laughing. "I've got something
special to show you!"

Giselle's room was full of snow
white ribbons and sparkling jewels. Hanging
up was a beautiful white dress.
"Ooh!" whispered Lettice.

Suddenly the dress twitched. Lettice stared as two hands appeared.

A boy scrambled out from under the dress. "This is Harry. He's going to be my ring bearer at the wedding," said Giselle.

"Harry," said Giselle, "at my wedding, I'd like you to carry my ring on this cushion."

Then she gave Lettice a basket and explained, "You will scatter flowers in front of me as I walk down the aisle."

Next, Lettice was measured for
her dress. "It'll be made especially
for you," said Giselle.

Lettice raced home with an invitation
for the whole family. She couldn't
wait to tell everyone about
the wedding.

On the morning of the wedding
Lettice woke up very early.

Her mother got the little ones
ready.

Lettice hopped across the meadow, gathering the prettiest flowers for her basket.

Giselle looked beautiful in her wedding dress.

"Harry," said Giselle, "here is the ring. Don't lose it!"

"Come with me, Lettice," she said, smiling. "It's time for you to put on your flower-girl dress."

Gently, Lettice unwrapped her clothes. "Just for me?" she whispered.

First she wiggled into the petticoat . . .

then she tied the ribbons on her slippers . . .

and placed some flowers on her ears.
Finally Lettice put on her new dress.

"Now I really am a flower girl!" she
sighed, swishing the skirt.

At last it was time for the wedding to begin.

Lettice took a deep breath and scattered her flowers.

They flew up in a colorful cloud.

As Giselle walked by, Lettice waited for Harry.

But Harry looked very worried.
"The ring!" he gasped.
"It's GONE!"
Lettice couldn't believe her ears.

Quickly, they searched along the path . . .

and all through the flowers. Harry began to cry.

Just as he pulled out his handkerchief,
Lettice saw something shining.

"The ring!" she shrieked. "It must have slipped into your
pocket! Quickly, we must catch up with Giselle!"

George beamed with happiness as he saw his
bride arrive with Lettice and Harry.

And when Giselle said, "I do," everyone sighed. It was the most beautiful wedding they had ever seen.

Later Giselle had presents for Lettice and Harry.
"I want to thank you both for helping to make this the
happiest day of my life," she said.

"And I have a present for you," said Lettice.
She twirled and whirled . . .

and

spun around in her own special dance, just for Giselle.

The moon was up by the time Lettice and her family
set off for home. Lettice was so tired that her father
had to carry her to their burrow.

"It's been a perfect day," she said sleepily. "The most perfect day of my life."